BLINDS

A MINDFUL POETRY COLLECTION

JARED PETERSON

SCYFTBOLD ENTERTAINMENT

To the Three Gates:

Desirelessness,
Formlessness,
Emptiness.

CONTENTS

INTRODUCTION

Desireless. Formless. Empty.

These were the three intentions I had in mind when I sat down March of 2024 in the hopes of *liking* writing again.

I had slipped into the bad habit of expectation and perfection every time I sat to write prose, but at a prompt from Beth Kempton's *The Way of the Fearless Writer*, I decided to start that March--not with the current novel project--but with a haiku.

Three simple lines. Easy. With just one haiku, the fire began to return, poetry a welcome asylum from the meandering tyranny of prose.

This collection, *Blinds*, is the best of this

poetry, both haiku and freeform It's been edited and critiqued since then, of course, but the essence remains the same--a series deeply connected to the moments in which each was written, and which demonstrate deeper truths through every-day imagery.

I was pleasantly surprised with what beauty I was able to allow through me as I deliberately entered these three gates. It is my great pleasure to share this beauty with you now, and to invite you to pass through these gates with me: Into a mindful space of desire-lessness, formlessness, and emptiness; a space of peace and love; a space of *joy*.

RESISTANCE

The rule,
If there are to be rules here,
Is to write the
Concrete.

But my questions today,
My curiosities,
Lie in the mind.

My mind, anyway.

That vacuous setting,
That Final Frontier
Where

Abstract is the rule.

Yet measured with a ruler,
Properly examined,
Ceases to leave any meaning
  behind.

As though meaning only comes
From the
Supernova flicker of candle
  flame, and
The hum-flick of piano in
  my ear.

The rule,
Maybe,
Isn't concrete at all.

It's now.

BLINDS

Stripes
Of light and shadow.

Fade fast,
Contrast faster,
Over linen cushions.

Possibility.

Dream-caught
Between nylon string.

SPILLED I

Hot stains everywhere.
Blue t-shirt, once-peach short-
shorts.
Sofa peed itself.

LITTLE

Open blue pencil box
Decorates the red couch arm.
Resting, as though waiting,
For little hands.

Little hands that left
Chapstick on the piano.
Pencil to its left,
Cereal box on dining-room
    table.

Maybe these socks are theirs,
    too:
Crumpled by the front door.
Waiting

For little hands
To put them on little feet
And get going
All over again.

DEVELOPMENT

Red
China-box
Light.

Not a district.
Not even a metaphor.

Just
A darkroom
Development

Over teriyaki chicken and
Super greens
Now brown and yellow.

LANDSCAPE

On a television screen.
Enormous, flat,
Big enough to be a painting.
If paintings moved.

A landscape:
Trail misted over;
Green-and-blue
Wildflowers
In a moor;
Fog swallows
Elden firs.

Over it all:

Grainy film,
Edit-suite static,
Simulates the old.

TYPEWRITERS

Portable
Antique
On an antiqued
Shelf.

Black-and-red ribbon lips
And striking silver teeth
Smile to the
Other one.

Across the room,
On the table.

Coquettish wink

From decor
To decoration.

SAVINGS

Slate and birdsong hide
Delayed daylight, shy shadows.

Robbed eyes find color.

MATTE

White acrylic—
Hazy Prussian—
Chisel-scrape
The sides of the sky.

Paint thinner and
Feathers brush
Up and up and up.

ANTICIPATION

Fingers (dawn's fingers)
Stretch, like the
Naked body that
Knows only gooseflesh—
Lusty ripples
Made from the
Pleasure of in-between:
That liminal heat,
Where contrast makes our
    meaning
And anticipation
Our content.

RAVEN

Corner lamp,
Raven's shadow
Pecks blue-line paper

Until words appear.

PORCELAIN

Two porcelain birds
Stare into a far distance.
"What're you thinking?"

HOMEWORK

*"Are you doing your
 homework?"*

*Startle.
Pen lifts off paper:
College-ruled, spiral notebook.*

*"No," you say.
"Just some journaling."*

*A half-smile,
A look away.
Gurgle of cooler water as she
Fills a pink Stanley.*

UNIQUECORN

It has pink fur
("It" because—)
And red-tipped ears.
(well, not sure if...)
Heart-shaped nostrils,
(do unicorns have gender?)
Pudgy little feet,
(Because isn't that the point?)
And caput cum cornu that
(Uniquecorn = possibility,)
Drills into the ground.
(a gender liminality,)
Inanimate,
(undefined)

Until the dogs come;
(by its own singularity.)
Then it's alive
(Empty projection.)
As it'll ever be.

SPILLED II

Sorry wet-glass eyes:
An apology of sorts.
All a dog can say.

STILL-LIFE

Ikea coffee table:
Wood-wick whiskey + oak,
Flat DP Zero,
Lily named Betty,
Sparkling cherry,
Candle holder
(no candle though),
Bath & Body balsam,
Drunk coffee dregs,
New remote,
Old remote,
Vinyl coasters,
Curled hair tie,
Shell-less iPhone.

(At least the table's cheap.)

CHAI

Black-pepper cardamom,
Unseen steam,
From mug lined orange
And warm, morning tea.

WEATHER

Quality of light today:
Clear,
Sunny, but
Blurred at the edges.

TECHNOLOGICAL

It's a reflection,
But there's no mirror.

The deep-gloss black
Of a dead-gloss screen.

Checking
Flipped realities.

Now on (1) writing;
Now on (0) self.

ABSOLUTE

OIOIOIII OIIIOOIO

OIIOIOOI OIIIOIOO

OIIOIOOI OIIOIIIO

OIIOOIII OOIIIIOI

OIOIOOII OIIOOIOI

OIIOIIOO OIIOOIIO

3,200 B.C.E.

Stylus in clay,
Now a stone-age tablet,
Technology reduced to
A hard surface for a notepad,
Case dresses it like a notebook:
The MacBook closed on my lap.

MONSTRUM

She stands
Still.

Patient, unmoving as
The earth she's implanted.

Spread-tooth jaws,
Leaf-broad heads.

She is:
Monster,
Monstera,
Monstrum.

CEE

Coconut air freshener,
Caramel coffee,
Cloudy conundrum.

Copper-painted centerpiece,
Clear-cut magnolia,
Cable television playing—

Cab rebuilds,
Capable mechanics,
Callous caddies.

BATHING

Banana-bread crumbs.
Fork, job done, now sunbathing
On the breakfast plate.

FISSION

Stare at the sun now.
Go on; it cannot hurt you
Blanketed in mist.

HEART

Bruised twilight.
Pinkish dawn.
Silhouetted movement.

Next (last) body part.
Length inside me, hour ago—
Now dressed—teases me.

AGAIN,

It starts with
Tacos;

He's been waiting,
And when he sees me,
He smiles;

Don't know yet this will turn,
Like the coming autumn,
Into packed-up apartment(s);

Then on, to a trail
Of haunted houses
Under moonlight,

FOREVER...

Midnight:
the color of his gaze;

His eyes, his sight,
I trust implicitly—
My own eyes strapped behind a
*   blindfold,*
High on a beer I never knew I
*   liked;*

Clothes bread-crumb a hotel
*   floor,*
Flow into a fog-mountain pool;

There I think I know,

I know,
This isn't just now;

No, his moonlight gaze
Stretches for miles,
Like sand
On an Oceanside
Beach—

Where maybe there's a
Cottage,
Conservatory,
Addendum:

Built to hold again
And again and
Again, forever...

SPILLED III

There they are, those stains.
Thrust at the end, the climax—
The rasped: "I love you."

CURTAIN

(Inter)*play:*

Splays of rain-light through
Bulging clouds:
Cotton-soft gray-light
From blinds blinded by

"Lights?"

Check.

Scene set.

For the players to come out
Of dressing rooms.

REVIEWS

Reviews are critical to boosting a piece's visibility and credibility. If you enjoyed this collection, please consider leaving a rating or review on the collection's page.

ABOUT THE AUTHOR

Jared Peterson mainly writes speculative fiction, with an emphasis on horror, thriller, and suspense. *Blinds* is his first foray into poetry. To keep up on Jared Peterson works, you can click the +Follow button on his Amazon author page.